It was early morning in the Llama Park. The ripe orange sun, already aglow in a bold blue sky, promised a hot lazy day.

The animals had just finished their breakfast and were either stretched out on their cool straw beds or fast asleep under the shade of the old oak tree. All of the animals that is, except for Snowy the mischievous llama.

As usual, Snowy was outside of the barn full of energy and dying to escape. Ever eager for adventure, he was determined to have one that very day.

Snowy was talking to his best friend, Lenny the lamb, about going to London.

Standing nearby was Gordon the goat who was listening to Snowy and Lenny's private conversation. "Llamas can't go to London," he announced suddenly in a haughty voice.

"I am going to London," Snowy said again.

"But I've told you, you can't go," Gordon the goat said once more.

"Why can't I?" Snowy asked.

"Just because llamas can't go to London, that's why?"

"But I want to know why?"

"Because I won't let you."

"Oh! yes I can. You can't stop me."

"Why do you want to go to London?" Lenny asked.

"Because I heard Fred the keeper saying that London was so exciting. It's Fred's day off today and he's going."

"Oh! I wish I could go," Lenny sighed, "but I'm not clever like you, Snowy. You can jump any fence, undo any gate. You can do anything you want. You're a super-llama."

"Yes! I am, aren't I? Besides, it's such a lovely day. Just the right-sort-of-day-for-escaping. Just the right-sort-of-day-for-sight-seeing."

"How will you get there?" Lenny asked.

"Oh! That's easy. I'll borrow Fred's old bike. He won't need it," Snowy replied.

"I've told you llamas can't go to London," Gordon the goat sniffed again in a lofty manner, "and llamas certainly can't ride bikes."

"But I can," Snowy said, "I'm a super-llama and I will."

Then, with a little laugh, Snowy hopped over the fence and climbed onto Fred's old bike. But it was no good. Snowy's body was too big and bulky and his legs were too stiff to turn the pedals. Not only that, he decided the bike would be too slow.

"No!" thought Snowy. "I must find something faster than that old bike."

"I told you llamas can't ride bikes," Gordon shouted out with glee.

"I'll show him," Snowy muttered to himself as he looked around. It was then he saw something black, red and shiny. It was a motorbike propped up against the fence.

"Hmmm! That'll go fast," Snowy said. "I'll borrow that instead. I've always wanted to ride a motorbike."

"But llamas can't ride motorbikes," Gordon shouted again, "and you must not."

"I can! You can't stop me. I'm a super-llama," Snowy replied.

Gordon and Lenny watched in amazement as Snowy climbed onto the leather seat.

It was very comfortable and Snowy's hooves just rested on the bodywork.

"Now! How does this thing start?"

He found the ignition key and pressed it. The engine burst into life with a loud *brrr brrr brrr*! Bubbling with excitement, Snowy and the bike roared up the path. He was so excited he didn't notice the two stowaway worms, Sid and Les, tucked snugly under his tail.

"Bye Snowy, have a good time," Lenny called out.

But a disgusted Gordon yelled, "That Snowy'll come a cropper one of these days."

Just at that moment, Maurie the milkman opened the gate to deliver the milk to the coffee shop.

"Now we'll see," Gordon said gleefully.

But it wasn't Snowy who came a cropper. It was Maurie. He was so surprised he couldn't believe his eyes. He had to jump quickly out of the way as Snowy roared past.

Picking himself up, Maurie shook his fist angrily and yelled out, "Llamas can't ride motorbikes."

"I can, I'm a super-llama," yelled Snowy.

"Do you know, I'm sure I saw a llama on a motorbike just now, or I'm a teacake," Maurie said to Betty in the coffee shop.

"You must be a teacake," Betty murmured. "Everyone knows a llama can't ride a motorbike."

When Snowy reached the end of the path, he saw his old friend Ferdy Fox.

"Which way shall I go, Ferdy?"

"Depends where you want to be, Eastbourne or Croydon?"

"I want to go to London."

"Llamas can't go to London."

"I can. I'm a super-llama."

"In that case turn right, then straight up the road to Croydon. There you'll catch a train."

"Thanks, Ferdy."

A farmer's wife who was going to the Llama Park with her friend had a surprise when Snowy passed by. She cried, "Did you see that? I'm sure it was a llama on a motorbike, or I'm a currant bun."

Her friend who was reading the notice board replied, "You must be a currant bun. Everyone knows llamas can't ride motorbikes."

"But I can. I'm a super-llama," Snowy yelled back.

Snowy was so excited that he didn't notice two cats, and a mouse called Montgomery, following him to join in on the big London adventure.

Snowy loved speeding along on the bike. But everyone he passed got the shock of their lives when they saw him. Even the people in buses, cars and coaches.

An American visitor on one coach asked the driver, "Do you usually have llamas on motorbikes in your country?"

"Search me!" the shocked driver replied, "First time I've seen it, Missus."

At the station Snowy parked the bike before going to the ticket office.

The station clerk was so surprised when Snowy asked for a ticket to London that he forgot to ask Snowy or his friends for the money.

It was just as well, as they did not have any.

"'Ere, llamas can't go on trains," the ticket collector said as he tried to stop Snowy. But Snowy just popped his ticket into the slot of the turnstile and trotted through the open gates to the platforms.

"I can, I've got a ticket. I'm a super-llama and you can't stop me."

The passengers on the train were so surprised when Snowy got on, they sat open-mouthed all the way to London.

"London Victoria, you're now at London Victoria," the voice on the train announced.

Snowy hopped off and trotted smartly through the station. The crowds of people on the forecourt were so surprised, they all shouted, "Llamas can't ride on trains, can they?" "Llamas can't come to London, can they?"

"But I can. I'm a super-llama," Snowy shouted in return.

Waiting outside was a special red bus. It had no roof. It was a sightseeing bus.

"'Ere you! Get off! Llamas can't go sightseeing," the driver yelled as Snowy hopped on the bus.

"I can, I'm a super-llama and you can't stop me," Snowy called back.

The happy but surprised passengers all nodded their heads wisely and said, "Yes! He can. Give him an all day ticket."

Now Snowy could ride round and round London.

The first stop was Buckingham Palace where Snowy waved to the Queen.

The Queen was so surprised to see a llama, she called out to Charles, "Oh! Do look Charles. There's a lovely llama on the sightseeing bus. Give him a wave."

Even the Queen gave him a wave.

Then when the military band marched down the Mall
with one man short...

...Snowy joined them and marched behind with the big base drum.
Boom! Boom! Boom! Boom! What a din!

19

Next he was in Trafalgar Square.

Snowy was so excited to see such a famous place. He did a little tap-dance with the pigeons. A crowd of people stopped to watch him.

Even Lord Nelson got down from his statue to watch. He said it was the best thing that had ever happened to him since he fought in the Battle of Trafalgar in 1805.

21

But when he got to the London Eye, Snowy was so excited he jumped right through the middle of the wheel. Just like an Olympic high-jumper. Snowy, who didn't like water, didn't realise that the River Thames was on the other side.

A poor man watching was so surprised, he fell into the river with shock.

"*Help! Help!*" yelled the man in the water.

"I can't swim! *Gurgle! Gurgle!*"

The people watching yelled, "*Help! Help!* He can't swim. He'll drown. What shall we do?" just as Snowy splashed into the water.

23

Overcoming his fear of water, Snowy swam to the man.

"Hold on to me," Snowy called out.

The man took hold of Snowy's long woolly coat and swam with Snowy to the river bank.

"Oh! Thank you for saving me! You're a hero," the grateful man said. He had forgotten it was Snowy's fault in the first place.

"*Hooray!* Hooray for the hero," the watching crowd cheered as they patted Snowy on the back.

"Yes! I am a hero, aren't I? I'm a super-hero," Snowy said as he trotted away to catch the bus.

When Snowy got off the bus at Covent Garden he saw a crowd of people watching a busker juggling. When the busker had finished, the crowd threw lots of money onto a plate. That gave Snowy an idea.

26

Borrowing the radio and microphone from the busker, he started to sing. The astonished crowd stopped to listen as Snowy's beautiful llama voice rang out with,

'Maybe it's because I'm a super-llama,
That I love London Town.'

After he had finished the crowd all shouted,
"That can't be a llama. Llamas can't sing like that can they?"

"I can," warbled Snowy, "I'm a super-llama." And he sang all over again.

Oh! How the people loved him They loved him so much, they threw lots of money onto a plate.

A little girl, called Poppy, collected the money in a purse. "Here you are," she said. And with a kiss hung it on a cord around his long woolly neck.

Snowy was so excited he simply bubbled with happiness. He had seen everything and done everything. There was nothing more he wanted to do.

But what was that strange sound coming from his tummy? A sort of rumbling like thunder. It was hunger. Snowy was hungry.

In fact he was very, very hungry indeed. Snowy realised he had not eaten since early that morning. He looked around to see if anyone could tell him where to get some food. But the crowd had gone and Snowy was all alone with no one to help him.

He thought of his friends at the Llama Park. They would be having their afternoon tea now.

Rumble! Rumble! his tummy grumbled again. *Rumble! Rumble!*

"Oh! Dear! I'm so hungry. I'll starve if I don't get something to eat," he cried. "What shall I do?"

Suddenly he was missing the Llama Park and all his friends. He felt very lonely. London had lost its excitement. What was he to do? Where was he to go?

Just then a friendly alley cat passed by.

"Please can you tell me where I can get some food?" Snowy asked the alley cat.

"Yes Sir! You've come to the right person. It just happens I can. Let me introduce myself. I'm Fritz and I dine at The Ritz. The Ritz has the best dustbins in town you know. Everything clean and wrapped. Just you go round the back."

And with a pussy smile Fritz disappeared round the corner.

"Thank you very much," Snowy called after him. Then rushing to the corner he shouted, "But Fritz! What is The Ritz?"

"It's an hotel," Fritz called back.

"But where is it? And how will I get there?"

"Just catch the bus to Piccadilly. You can't miss The Ritz. Everyone knows it."

But did Snowy go round the back? No! He went to the front.

"Here you! Llamas can't go in The Ritz," Haughty Henry, the posh doorman said as he barred Snowy's way.

"But I can, I'm a hero and a super singer. I sang in Covent Garden and I'm very, very rich."

"You sang at Covent Garden!" Henry the doorman was very impressed. "Follow me to the Palm Court. The head waiter will show you to your table. All the great singers have tea in the Palm Court."

When told that Snowy, a hero and great singer, had just sung at Covent Garden, the head waiter said, "Follow me. For you, a hero and great singer, the very best table. All the great singers from Covent Garden sit here for our special tea. We've had Parrotpotty, Plassydingo, and even the great Caber-rhinoceros," the head waiter said as he handed Snowy the menu.

Oh! How Snowy enjoyed his tea as waiters in long black morning coats came to serve him. Everyone thought Snowy had sung in the grand opera house. They didn't know it was only on the pavement in the Covent Garden market place

Huge platters of delicious food were carried in. And a greedy Snowy gobbled the lot. He gobbled his way through fifty different kinds of dainty sandwiches, fifty different kinds of cheese scones, fifty plain scones with different kinds of jam and cream, and fifty different kinds of fancy cakes. He washed the lot down with fifty pots of Earl Grey tea.

The waiters looked on in awe and great admiration. They had never seen such a huge appetite before. Even the managing director of The Ritz came down to watch.

By the time Snowy had finished, word had got around London about the great singer and super-hero. Newspaper reporters, television cameras and a great crowd of people were gathered outside the hotel chanting "We want Snowy the great singer, we want Snowy the super-hero."

A lot of the people even came in for tea. The hotel was so full there was a huge queue waiting.

The managers of The Ritz were very impressed. They began to call Snowy 'Sir Snowy'. And when Sir Snowy was ready, they sent for a big black car to take him home. Sir Snowy climbed onto the back seat. It was so soft and comfortable. It was so luxurious and splendid. It was so exciting. He felt like a king. Looking out of the window he raised his hoof and waved a kingly wave to the crowd. The people went mad with joy.

"Hooray for Sir Snowy the Great Hero!" they cheered.

"Hooray for Sir Snowy the Great Singer!"

But there was one person standing outside The Ritz who was wondering what all the fuss was about.

It was Fred the keeper from the Llama Park. He had just come along to see why there was such a huge crowd.

"What's going on?" Fred asked a man in the crowd. "Why are all these people and cameras here?"

"Don't you know? It's that famous singer from Covent Garden and he saved a man from drowning. He's just had his tea at The Ritz and now he's in that large black car," the man replied.

Fred looked across to where the man was pointing. And what a surprise he got. Fred was so surprised that his eyes nearly popped out of the top of his head. Puzzled, he scratched his forehead then yelled out, "That's no famous singer, that's no hero. That's Snowy our llama from the Llama Park. He must have escaped and followed me to London."

"Don't be silly!" the crowd yelled back. "Llamas can't come to London."

"But I can. I'm a Super-Llama and I *did*," Snowy called back happily as the big car moved off.

Who else got a lift home?

Snowy's Puzzles and Games...

... searching...

... amazing ...

... dotty ...

Snowy's Album

The Andes is a mountainous region on the western side of South America. That's why a warm coat is needed. The people are known as Pervvias who use the llamas to carry loads up to 25 kilograms.

Fred measuring me when I was full grown. As you can see I'm taller than Fred.

Me, as a youngster – 10 kgs. A young llama is known as a cria. My big ears give me a good sense of hearing and I use them to signal to my friends. I have a good sense of smell.

Not my best view, but it shows my woolly coat. I have another finer layer of wool underneath to keep me warm in the mountains.

My relatives live in South America in the three countries shown.

Oops! A picture of my foot. Not a hoof but two big toes and a soft pad to give me a good grip on rough stony ground.

What I like doing best of all - eating. Grass, grain and hay.

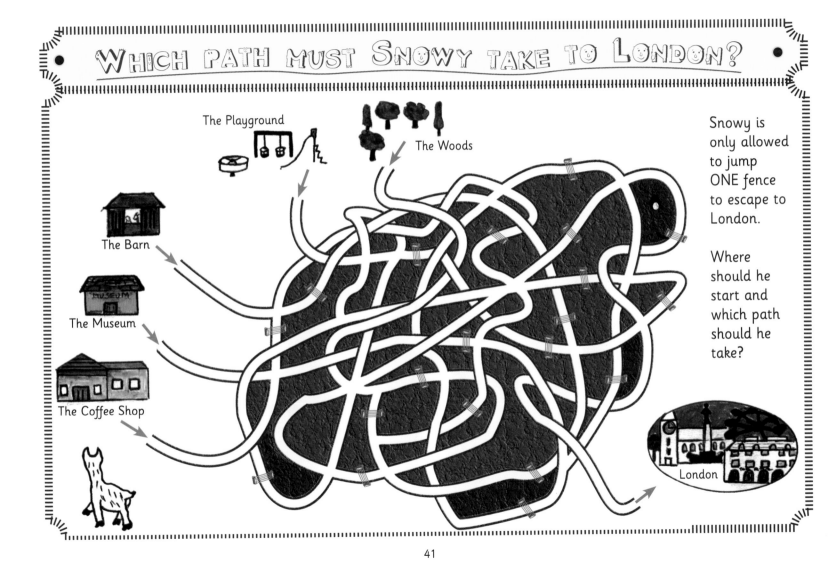

The Playground

The Woods

The Barn

The Museum

The Coffee Shop

London

Snowy is only allowed to jump ONE fence to escape to London.

Where should he start and which path should he take?

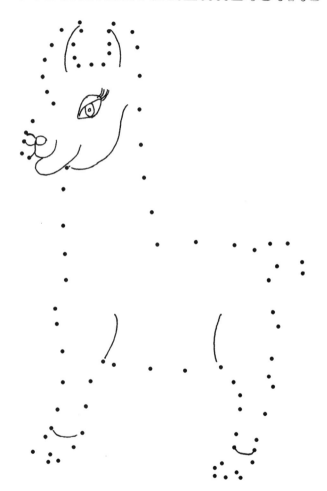

HIDDEN WORD

Using the picture clues, find the names of the characters in the story to reveal the hidden word.

SNOWY'S CROSSWORD PUZZLE

ACROSS:

1 The number of cakes Snowy had for tea. (5)

3 Wool comes from this famous animal. (5)

7 The line the crowd formed to wait for their tea at The Ritz. (5)

8 The purse was tied around Snowy's neck with this. (4)

10 Snowy used this to get to Croydon. (9)

13 Snowy became a celebrity, or a _ _ _ _. (4)

16 The name of The Ritz doorman. (5)

17 He travelled to London with the cats. (5)

18 The animals like to cool off under them. (5)

DOWN:

1 Snowy jumped this to escape. (5)

2 One of the car number plate numbers. (4)

4 How Snowy's drumming sounded. (4)

5 What the soldiers are swinging. (3)

6 What the crowd called Snowy. (5, 4)

9 The number of wheels on the juggler's bike. (3)

10 He fell in the water. (3)

11 What Snowy and the soldiers played in the Mall. (5)

12 The Ritz served lots of these to Snowy's admirers. (4)

14 What the clock tells. (4)

15 Snowy had different kinds of this with his tea. (3)

SNOWY'S WORDSEARCH

Find the words listed to the right. Remember, words can go left, right, up, down and sideways.
One word is repeated twice, but which one?

R	J	M	B	I	I	Q	Z	T	I	R	R	Q	M	Z
G	D	V	Z	B	L	Z	N	O	D	N	O	L	B	I
R	J	P	N	O	I	S	I	V	E	L	E	T	C	S
E	S	A	N	D	W	I	C	H	E	S	C	Q	T	U
O	K	K	C	M	C	O	X	U	N	E	H	A	N	K
A	T	A	L	N	E	L	S	O	N	W	R	E	C	H
K	M	I	C	O	W	O	W	O	S	T	E	K	Y	J
H	W	A	K	A	A	Y	H	B	E	K	L	I	N	R
M	Z	X	L	R	E	P	X	X	I	Z	G	B	S	J
M	V	I	E	L	O	T	E	B	I	Q	G	R	V	X
S	E	P	F	R	Y	D	R	E	F	T	U	O	J	W
M	O	C	C	H	R	O	A	M	I	Z	J	T	E	W
W	P	I	I	P	T	D	U	V	B	P	Z	O	P	B
U	M	A	U	O	T	Q	Q	N	R	A	B	M	Z	L
X	P	U	M	X	V	O	S	U	C	D	O	O	H	T

BARN
FERDY
JUGGLER
LLAMA
LONDON
MICROPHONE
MOTORBIKE
NELSON
OAK
OPERA
RITZ
SANDWICHES
SNOWY
SQUARE
STAR
TEACAKE
TELEVISION
VOICE

Snowy's Further Adventures...

... Create your own story

... Colour the pages

And you can add your own speech balloons too...

47

ESCAPE TO LONDON ... PAGE 41

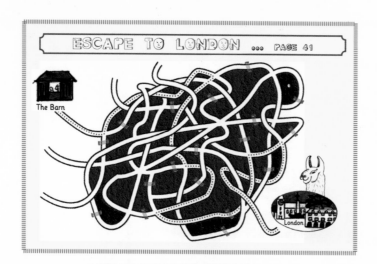

The Barn

London

HIDDEN WORD ... PAGE 42

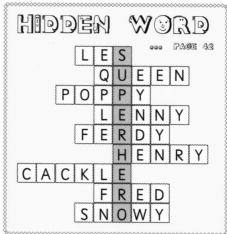

```
L E S
  Q U E E N
P O P P Y
  L E N N Y
  F E R D Y
    H E N R Y
C A C K L E
  F R E D
S N O W Y
```

SNOWY'S CROSSWORD

```
F I F T Y   L L A M A
E   O     S   O     R
N   U   Q U E U E   M
C O R D   P   D   O
E         E       N
    M O T O R B I K E
  A       H       D
  N   T   E   S T A R
J H E N R Y     I   U
A     A   O     M   M
M O U S E   T R E E S
```

... PAGE 43

Why does a llama make a good pet?

WORDSEARCH ... PAGE 44

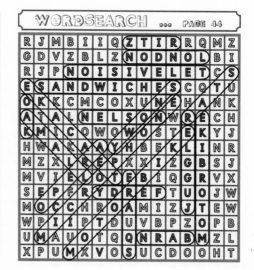

Because a llama wakes you up in the morning

62